The Book from the Black Lagoon

by Mike Thaler · pictures by Jared Lee

READ
IF YOU KNOW
WHAT'S GOOD
FOR YOU!

SCHOLASTIC INC.

New York   Toronto   London   Auckland   Sydney
Mexico City   New Delhi   Hong Kong   Buenos Aires

For Teryl Anne McLane
who reads between the lines
—M.T.

To all the cool kids who love our Black Lagoon books
—J.L.

This book is dedicated to our literacy partners—our loyal Book Fair
chairpeople and the millions of kids they reach every year.
—Scholastic Book Fairs

MRS. BEAMSTER, THE LIBRARIAN

ISBN 0-439-88348-2

Text copyright © 2006 by Mike Thaler.
Illustrations copyright © 2006 by Jared D. Lee Studio, Inc.

12 11 10 9 8 7 6 5 4 3 2 1   6 7 8 9 10 11/0

Printed in the U.S.A.
First printing, September 2006

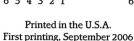

Mrs. Beamster, our librarian, says we're having a Book Fair.

I've heard a lot of weird things about it.

They say a big truck comes and dumps a ton of books into a closet.

Then they throw you in and won't let you out
until you buy some.

When your mom comes to pick you up after school, they chain her to the library wall and give her a badge that says, "Volunteer."

Then they invite the rest of your relatives and throw them in the closet with you.

The whole thing is run by a *chairperson*.

I wonder if that is anything like a *couch potato*?

They say the school makes a ton of money from the Book Fair
and that they use it to buy more devices to torture you with.

If you get out of the closet, you have to wear signs advertising the Book Fair. They're called "sandwich boards." They say things like: Read If You Know What's Good for You! and Buy or Else! I hope they leave the mayonnaise off of mine.

They lure the rest of the neighborhood in with food—donuts for dads, muffins for moms, nuts for neighbors.

WOW!

FREE FOOD

WHO SITS IN THE LIBRARY, HAS LOTS OF HAIR, AND GROWLS?

THE LIBEARIAN

WHAT REFERENCE BOOK DOES A PIG USE THE MOST?

THE PIGTIONARY

I HAVE FIVE STORIES.

I ONLY HAVE TIME TO READ ONE.

TRUCK TIRE

FRESH DONUT

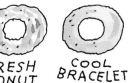

COOL BRACELET

HULA HOOP

MONSTER EYEBALL

COOKED EGG

 And they pick the worst dates ever, when all your favorite TV shows are on.

Mrs. Green, my teacher, is writing down a list of books she wants. It's 20 feet long. It's called a "Wish List" cause you'll wish you'd never seen it. If she doesn't get everything on it—the whole class fails.

Well, we're marching down the hall toward the library.

I'm scared. There are lots of signs and banners.

NO BITING

DON'T FEED THE BOOKS

THIS WAY

GOOD LUCK

WHAT MAKES YOU A CHAMPION? I HAVE A LOT OF TITLES.

WHY DOES A BOOK MAKE MUSIC? BECAUSE IT'S A READ INSTRUMENT.

WHY DID THE MONSTER EAT THE LIBRARY? HE WAS HUNGRY FOR KNOWLEDGE.

Here we are. Mom is here, too, but she's not chained to the wall. She's smiling and pointing to cases filled with books.

Wow! There are fairy tales and merry tales, mysteries and mice stories.

There are pirates and pilots, and dragons and dolphins.

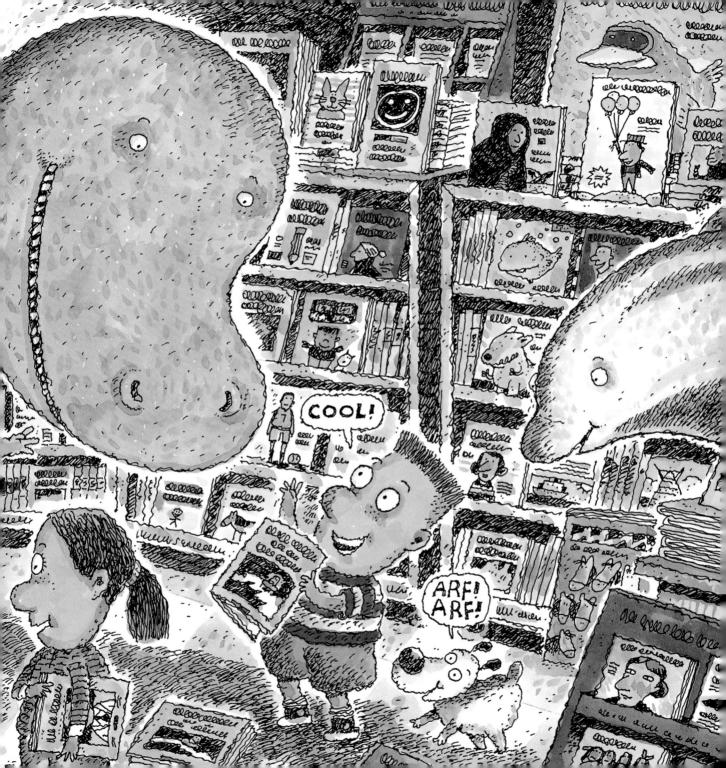

There are jesters and jugglers, wizards and lizards,
and all my favorite things!

Mom gives me ten dollars and a big red dog gives me a hug. Now I can buy books and start my *own* library at home.

I don't care what's on TV tonight . . . I'm booked for the evening.

Why do Jared and I like working with Scholastic Book Fairs? Well, first of all, we have fun together. These are people who enjoy their work. And that's because they believe in what they are doing—getting good books into the hands of kids. We are all on the same team—parents, teachers, librarians, principals, authors, illustrators, and Book Fairs.

We are a team with the same goals—to educate and inspire each succeeding generation. This is the reason we all love what we do.

Mike Thaler

10 Steps to Running a Successful Scholastic Book Fair

1. **Partner with your school principal.** Principal support is a key ingredient to a successful event.

2. **Find a large space for the Book Fair.** The bigger the space, the better. Keep in mind that many schools have 300-400 parents, students, and teachers during an afternoon or evening Book Fair event.

3. **Recruit plenty of volunteers to help plan, promote, and run the Fair.** The more volunteers, the better. Large Book Fairs often have co-chairs, who help organize and execute different elements of the event.

4. **Involve your teachers and students in promoting the Book Fair and creating excitement.** Have students make posters and decorate the school to let everyone know the Book Fair is coming.

5. **Get the whole school community excited about the Book Fair, books, and reading.** Set a minimum goal for the Fair to make sure every student participates and buys at least one book.

6. **Schedule a Teacher Preview.** Invite teachers to the Book Fair before it opens so they can select books they want for their classrooms. The books are displayed as part of the Classroom Wish List and then generous parents buy the books for teachers.

7. **Show the Author Video to students.** Students can meet some of their favorite authors and learn about books that will be at the Fair. It's a great way to get students reading.

8. **Schedule a time for all students to preview the Fair.** Have someone give a book talk for students to hear. This short speech about the book will generate excitement and interest among students.

9. **Plan events during the Fair to attract parents and grandparents.** Family Events, Donuts for Dads, and Muffins for Moms are great ways to get the whole family involved in the Fair.

10. **Ask the community to help buy books for classrooms and students.** Collect donations through the One for Books program.

After the event, celebrate, celebrate, and celebrate! YOU helped put books into the hands of kids. YOU helped acquire new books for classrooms. YOU got kids reading and YOU helped raise funds for your school!

Thanks!